For Scott and Nick — V.D.P.

For My Dad — B.M.

Brer Rabbit Jumps Again

JUMP

Again!

More Adventures of Brer Rabbit
BY JOEL CHANDLER HARRIS

ADAPTED BY VAN DYKE PARKS   *ILLUSTRATED BY* BARRY MOSER

Voyager Books
Harcourt Brace & Company
San Diego   New York   London

Requests for permission to make copies of any part of the work should be
mailed to: Permissions Department, Harcourt Brace & Company,
6277 Sea Harbor Drive, Orlando, Florida 32887-6777.

First Voyager Books edition 1997
Voyager Books is a registered trademark of Harcourt Brace & Company.

Library of Congress Cataloging-in-Publication Data
Parks, Van Dyke.
Jump again!
"Voyager Books."
Contents: Brer Rabbit, he's a good fisherman—the wonderful tar-baby story—
how Brer Weasel was caught—Brer Rabbit and the mosquitoes—[etc.]
1. Afro-Americans—Folklore. 2. Tales—Southern States. [1. Folklore,
Afro-Americans. 2. Animals—Folklore.] I. Harris, Joel Chandler,
1848–1908. II. Moser, Barry, ill. III. Title.
PZ8.1.P2255Jum 1987 398.2'452 86-33622
ISBN 0-15-241352-9
ISBN 0-15-201559-0 pb

F E D C B A

Printed in Singapore

Special thanks to Malcolm Jones for his contributions to *Jump!*

The illustrations in this book, both color and black-and-white, were executed with watercolor
on paper handmade for the Royal Watercolor Society in 1982 by J. Barcham Greene.
The text type and display type were set in Cochin by Thompson Type, San Diego, California.
The calligraphy was done by Reassurance Wunder, West Hatfield, Massachusetts.
Color separations by Bright Arts, Ltd., Singapore
Printed and bound by Tien Wah Press, Singapore
This book was printed on Leykam recycled paper, which contains more than 20 percent
postconsumer waste and has a total recycled content of at least 50 percent.
Production supervision by Stanley Redfern and Jane Van Gelder
Designed by Barry Moser

Contents

Storyteller's Note

The folktales in this book have been told and retold for so many years, and in so many countries, that their history is uncertain and difficult to trace. Whatever their origin, we know these stories were brought to the American South by black slaves who came to the United States against their will. Brer Rabbit, a seemingly defenseless creature who regularly outsmarts much bigger animals, reminds us that resourcefulness and courage have the power to overcome ignorance and brute strength.

Throughout his life, Joel Chandler Harris, a Georgian newspaperman, insisted that he was merely the "compiler" and not the creator of these stories. He gathered them from Southern blacks in the late 1800s and published them in a book called *Uncle Remus: His Songs and His Sayings,* the first of several collections. Harris invented a character named Uncle Remus, an elderly black plantation slave who told stories about Brer Rabbit and his friends to a little white boy.

Neither Harris nor Remus ever claimed to know the chronological sequence of the events in the Brer Rabbit adventures. In some tales, for example, Brer Rabbit struggles to support and protect his wife and children, while in others he is a lighthearted bachelor in love. When the little boy questions this, Remus explains that this is the way the tales were told to *him.*

Harris has been both applauded and deeply criticized for his use of dialect and his portrayal of life in the Old South. Yet the tales themselves never fail to reflect the power of the human spirit. *Jump!* and *Jump Again!* bring a timeless hero to a new generation of readers. As Brer Rabbit says, "There's always a way, if not two."

—V.D.P.

WAY back yonder — it might have been in the year One for all we
know — Brer Rabbit could cut more capers than a hive has bumbly-bees.

Under his hat, Brer Rabbit had a mighty quick thinking apparatus,
and all the time, the pranks he played on the other folks pestered them
both ways — a-coming and a-going.

In those days, Brer Rabbit and Brer Fox were like a couple of little
children. Both of them were always after one another, playing pranks and
romancing around, and nobody got a minute's peace. Brer Fox did all he
could to catch Brer Rabbit, and Brer Rabbit did all he could to keep him
from it. But there came a time when the folks kept getting more familiar

with one another until by and by, they decided to get their provisions planted together.

One day, when Brer Rabbit and Brer Fox and Brer Coon and Brer Bear and a whole lot of the folks were clearing up new ground to plant a roasting-ear patch, the sun got to be sort of hot, and Brer Rabbit, he got tired. But he didn't let on, because he feared the rest of them would call him lazy.

He just kept on toting off trash and piling up brush until by and by, he hollered out that he got a briar stuck in his hand. Then he skipped off and hunted for a cool place to rest. After a while, he came across a well with a bucket hanging in it.

"That looks cool," said Brer Rabbit, said he, "and cool I expect it is. I think I'll just get in there and take a nap." And with that, in he jumped, and he no sooner fixed himself in the bucket than the bucket began to go down.

Well, there hasn't been a worse scared beast since the world began than this Brer Rabbit. He fairly had a heart attack. He knew where he came from, but he didn't know where he was going.

Directly, he felt the bucket hit the water, and there it sat. Brer Rabbit, he kept mighty still, because he didn't know what minute was going to be his last. He just lay there and shook and shivered.

But as you well know, Brer Fox always had one eye on Brer Rabbit. And when Brer Rabbit slipped off from the day's work, Brer Fox sneaked after him. He knew Brer Rabbit was after some project or another, and he took off, he did, and watched him.

Brer Fox saw Brer Rabbit come to the well and stop, and then he saw him go down out of sight. Brer Fox was the most astonished fox that you ever laid eyes on. He sat off there in the bushes and studied and studied, but he couldn't make head nor tail of this kind of business.

Then he said to himself, "Well, if this doesn't bang my times," said he, "then Joe's dead and Sal's a widow. Right down there in that well, Brer Rabbit keeps his money hidden, and if that isn't it, then he's gone and discovered a gold mine. And if it isn't that, then I'm going to see what it is."

Brer Fox crept up a little closer, he did, and listened. But he didn't hear any fuss, so he kept on getting closer. Yet he still didn't hear any-

Brer Rabbit & Brer Fox in the Well

thing. All this time Brer Rabbit was mighty near to being scared out of his skin, and he was afraid to move because the bucket might keel over and spill him out into the water.

While he was saying his prayers over and over like a train of cars running, old Brer Fox hollered out, "Heyo, Brer Rabbit! Who are you visiting down there?" said he.

"Who? Me? Oh, I'm just fishing, Brer Fox," said Brer Rabbit, said he. "I just told myself that I'd sort of surprise you all with a mess of fishes for dinner, so here I am, and there are the fishes. I'm fishing for suckers, Brer Fox."

"Are there many of them down there, Brer Rabbit?" said Brer Fox.

"Lots of them, Brer Fox; scores and scores of them. The water is alive with them. Come down and help me haul them in, Brer Fox," said Brer Rabbit.

"How am I going to get down, Brer Rabbit?"

"Jump into the bucket, Brer Fox. It'll fetch you down all safe and sound."

Brer Rabbit talked so happily and talked so sweet that Brer Fox, he jumped in the bucket, he did, and as he went down, of course his weight pulled Brer Rabbit up.

When they passed one another at the halfway point, Brer Rabbit sang out:

Good-bye, Brer Fox, take care of your clothes,
For this is the way the world goes;
Some go up and some go down;
You'll get to the bottom all safe and sound.

When Brer Rabbit got out, he galloped off for home, and when he got there, he flung both hands over his face. From the way he looked, you'd have thought his heart was broken; yet he wasn't crying. He was just laughing so bad it hurt him to laugh, and then he laughed some more for good measure.

As for Brer Fox, he scrambled and scuffled until he got out of that well, he did, and he stood there and kind of shook himself because he was mighty glad to find that he was in the world once more — even though he was feeling kind of sheepish and just a might wet behind the ears.

The Tar-Baby

ON the day after Brer Rabbit fooled Brer Fox in the well, Brer Fox went to work and fixed up a contraption that he called a Tar-Baby. He took that Tar-Baby, and he sat her in the big road, and then he lay off in the bushes to see what the news was going to be. He didn't have to wait long, because by and by, there came Brer Rabbit pacing down the road — lippity-clippity, clippity-lippity — just as sassy as a jaybird.

Brer Fox, he lay low.

Brer Rabbit came prancing along until he spied the Tar-Baby, and then he stood up on his hind legs like he was astonished.

The Tar-Baby, she sat there, she did.

"Morning!" said Brer Rabbit. "Nice weather today," said he.

Tar-Baby didn't say anything, and Brer Fox, he lay low.

"How do?" said Brer Rabbit.

Brer Fox, he winked his eye slow, and the Tar-Baby, she wasn't saying anything.

Brer Rabbit, All Stuck Up

"How are you coming on then? Are you deaf?" said Brer Rabbit. "Because if you are, I can holler louder," said he.

Tar-Baby stayed still, and Brer Fox, he lay low.

"You are stuck up, that's what you are," said Brer Rabbit, "and I'm going to cure you, that's what I'm going to do," said he.

Brer Fox, he sort of chuckled in his stomach, he did, but Tar-Baby wasn't saying anything.

"I'm going to teach you how to talk to respectable folks if it's my last act," said Brer Rabbit, said he. "If you don't take off that hat and say howdy, I'm going to bust you wide open."

Tar-Baby stayed still, and Brer Fox, he lay low.

Brer Rabbit, he kept on asking, and Tar-Baby, she kept on saying nothing, until presently Brer Rabbit drew back with his fist, he did, and blipped her on the side of her head.

Right there is where he broke his molasses jug. His fist stuck, and he couldn't pull it loose. The tar held him. But Tar-Baby, she wasn't saying anything, and Brer Fox, he lay low.

"Turn me loose, before I kick the natural stuffing out of you," said Brer Rabbit, said he, but Tar-Baby, she wasn't saying anything. She just held on, and then Brer Rabbit lost the use of his feet in the same way.

Then Brer Rabbit squalled out that if Tar-Baby didn't turn him loose, he'd butt her cranksided. And then he butted, and his head got stuck.

Then Brer Fox, he sauntered forth, looking as innocent as one of your mother's mockingbirds.

"Howdy, Brer Rabbit," said Brer Fox, said he. "You look sort of stuck up this morning," said he, and then he rolled on the ground and laughed and laughed until he could laugh no more, with his teeth all white and shiny, like they were brand-new.

"I expect you'll be having dinner with me this time, Brer Rabbit. I done fished up some suckers myself from that there well yesterday, and I ain't going to take no excuse," said Brer Fox, said he.

He felt mighty good, and by and by he up and said, "Well, I got you this time, Brer Rabbit," said he. "Maybe I ain't, but I expect I have. You've been running around here sassing after me a mighty long time, but now you've done come to the end of the row. You've been cutting up

Brer Fox, Lost in Thought

your capers and bouncing around this neighborhood until you've come to believe you're the boss of the whole gang. And then you're always somewhere where you've got no business."

And then Brer Fox said, said he, "Who asked you to come and strike up an acquaintance with this here Tar-Baby? And who stuck you up there where you are? Nobody in the round world. You just threw yourself on that Tar-Baby without waiting for any invitation," said he, "and there you are, and there you'll stay until I fix up a brush-pile and fire it up, because I'm going to barbecue you this day for sure."

Then Brer Rabbit talked mighty humble.

"I don't care what you do with me, Brer Fox," said he, "so long as you don't fling me in that briar patch."

"It's so much trouble to kindle a fire," said Brer Fox, "that I expect I'll have to hang you."

"Hang me just as high as you please, Brer Fox," said Brer Rabbit, said he, "but for the sake of heaven, don't fling me in that briar patch."

"I don't have any string," said Brer Fox, "and now I expect I'll have to drown you."

"Drown me just as deep as you please, Brer Fox," said Brer Rabbit, "but don't fling me in that briar patch."

"There isn't any water nearby," said Brer Fox, "and now I expect I'll have to skin you."

"Skin me, Brer Fox," said Brer Rabbit, said he, "snatch out my eyeballs, tear out my ears by the roots, and cut off my legs," said he, "but please, Brer Fox, don't fling me in that briar patch."

Of course Brer Fox wanted to hurt Brer Rabbit as bad as he could, so he caught him up and flung him into the middle of the briar patch. There was a considerable flutter where Brer Rabbit struck the bushes, and Brer Fox sort of hung around to see what was going to happen.

By and by, he heard somebody call him, and way up the hill he saw Brer Rabbit sitting cross-legged on a chinquapin log, cleaning the tar out of his hair with a comb. Then Brer Fox knew he'd been fooled mighty bad.

Brer Rabbit, he opened up with a big *ha ha ha* so loud it made the other folks take to the bushes. He flung back his head and fetched out a

The Briar Patch

whoop that you could hear from here to Hominy Grove. It surely was scandalous, the way Brer Rabbit could laugh, and he couldn't help but throw back some of his own sass.

He hollered out, "I was bred and born in a briar patch, Brer Fox — bred and born in a briar patch! There's no place I love better!"

And with that, he skipped off as lively as a cricket in the embers.

Brer Weasel

t HERE were times when Brer Rabbit pushed folks so far they couldn't help but want to get even with him. Folks took after him, and they messed with him, and they tried to destroy him. But there were other times when folks couldn't help but call on him to help them out of their trouble.

There was one time when all the creatures were living in the same settlement and drinking out of the same spring, and it got so that they put all their butter together in the springhouse. Then they'd go off and tend to their business. But when they came back, they found that someone had been nibbling at their butter.

They took to hiding their butter all around in that springhouse. They set it up on the rafters, and they buried it in the sand. Yet all the same, the butter would be missing.

By and by, it got so bad they didn't know what to do. They examined the tracks, and they found out that the one who'd been nibbling their butter was Brer Weasel. He'd come in the night, he'd come in the day; they couldn't catch him.

At last the folks held a meeting, and they agreed that they had to set someone to watch so they could catch Brer Weasel.

Brer Mink, he was the first one appointed because he wasn't more than half a man, any way you looked at it. The other folks, they went off to their work, and Brer Mink, he wouldn't be missed while he sat up with the butter.

Brer Mink

He watched and he listened, he listened and he watched; he didn't see a thing, he didn't hear a thing. Yet he kept on watching, because the other folks went and made a rule that if Brer Weasel came while somebody was watching and got off without getting caught, the one who was watching couldn't eat any more butter for that whole year.

Brer Mink, he watched and he waited. He sat so still that by and by, he got cramps in his legs, and about that time, Brer Weasel popped his head under the door. He saw Brer Mink, and he hailed him.

"Heyo, Brer Mink! You look sort of lonesome in there. Come out here and let's play a game of hide-and-seek."

Brer Mink, he wanted to have some fun, he did, and he joined Brer Weasel in the game. They played and they played until by and by, Brer Mink got so worn out that he couldn't run scarcely, and as soon as they sat down to rest, Brer Mink, he dropped off to sleep.

Little Brer Weasel, so mighty proud and fine, he went and nibbled up the butter, and popped out the way he came in.

The folks, they came back, they did, and they found the butter nibbled and Brer Weasel gone. With that, they marked Brer Mink's name down, and he wasn't allowed to eat any more butter that year. Then they had another meeting and appointed Brer Possum to watch the butter.

Brer Possum, he grinned and watched upside-down, and by and by, sure enough, in popped Brer Weasel. He came in, he did, and he sort of poked Brer Possum in the short ribs and asked him how he was coming on. Brer Possum was mighty ticklish, and every time Brer Weasel poked him, he laughed harder. Brer Weasel kept on poking him that way until by and by, Brer Possum laughed himself plum out of wind, and Brer Weasel left him there and nibbled up the butter.

The folks, they marked Brer Possum's name down and appointed Brer Coon. Brer Coon, he started in mighty fine; but while he was sitting there, little Brer Weasel challenged him to a race up the branch.

No sooner said than there they went! Brer Coon, he followed the turns of the branch, but Brer Weasel, he took shortcuts, and in no time at all he'd won the race. Then they ran down the branch, and before Brer Coon could catch up with him, that Brer Weasel skedaddled back to the butter and nibbled it up.

Brer Fox & Brer Coon

Then the creatures marked Brer Coon's name down, they did, and appointed Brer Fox to watch the butter.

Now, Brer Weasel was sort of afraid of Brer Fox. He studied the situation a long time, and then he waited until night. Then he went around to the old field and woke up the Killdeer family and drove them toward the springhouse.

Brer Fox heard them holler, and it made his mouth water. By and by, he allowed to himself that there wouldn't be harm if he went out and slipped up on one.

Brer Fox, his name got marked down, and then the folks appointed Brer Wolf to be their watcher. Brer Wolf, he sat up there, he did, and sort of nodded, but by and by, he heard someone talking outside the springhouse.

He fixed up his ears to listen, and it looked like some of the folks were going by, talking amongst themselves.

"I wonder who put that young sheep down there by the chinquapin tree," somebody said. "I'd sure like to know why Brer Wolf isn't there yet."

Then it seemed like the folks passed on, and old Brer Wolf, his mouth watered so bad he forgot what he was there for, and he dashed down to the chinquapin tree to get the young sheep. But there wasn't a sheep there, and when he got back, he saw that Brer Weasel had been in there and nibbled the butter.

Then the folks marked Brer Wolf's name down and appointed Brer Bear to keep his eye upon the butter. Brer Bear, he sat up there, he did, and licked his paw, and felt good.

By and by, Brer Weasel came dancing in. He allowed, "You got any fleas on your back, Brer Bear?"

With that, Brer Weasel began to rub Brer Bear on the back and scratch him on the sides, and it wasn't long before Brer Bear was stretched out fast asleep and snoring like a sawmill. Of course, Brer Weasel got the butter. Brer Bear, he got his name marked down, and then the folks didn't scarcely know what to do.

Some said to send for Brer Rabbit, some said to send for Judge Buzzard, but at last they sent for Brer Rabbit.

Brer Possum

Brer Rabbit, he took a notion that they were fixing up some way to trick him, and they had to beg a mighty long time before he would come and watch their butter.

But by and by, he agreed, and he went down to the springhouse and looked around. Then he went and got a twine string and hid himself where he could keep his eye on the butter.

He didn't have to wait long for Brer Weasel. Just as he was about to nibble the butter, Brer Rabbit hollered out, "Let that butter alone!"

Brer Weasel jumped back like the butter burnt him. "Surely that must be Brer Rabbit!" he said, said he.

"The same. I allowed you'd know me. Just let that butter alone."

"Aw, let me get one little bitty taste, Brer Rabbit."

"Just let that butter alone."

Then Brer Weasel said he wanted to run a race. Brer Rabbit said he was tired. Brer Weasel allowed he wanted to play hide-and-seek. Brer Rabbit said that his hiding days were passed and gone. Brer Weasel bantered and bantered him, and by and by, Brer Rabbit came up with a banter of his own.

"I'll take and tie your tail," said he, "and you'll take and tie mine, and then we'll see which tail is stronger." Brer Weasel knew how weak Brer Rabbit's tail was, but he surely didn't know how strong Brer Rabbit was with his tricks. So they tied their tails with Brer Rabbit's twine string.

Brer Weasel was to stand inside, and Brer Rabbit was to stand outside, and they were to pull against one another with their tails. Brer Rabbit, he slipped out of the string and tied the end around a tree root, and then he went and peeped at Brer Weasel tugging and pulling.

By and by Brer Weasel allowed, "Come and untie me, Brer Rabbit, because you surely outpulled me."

Brer Rabbit sat there, he did, and took a chaw of rabbit tobacco and looked like he felt sorry about something. Yes sir, there isn't a smart man that won't find one smarter, and Brer Weasel's time had come.

By and by, all the folks came to see about their butter because they were afraid Brer Rabbit had run away with it. Yet when they saw Brer Weasel tied by the tail, they made great admiration about Brer Rabbit. And they allowed he was the smartest one of the whole gang.

Miss Wolf

JUST when it seemed like everything and everybody was running along so smoothly they must have had wagon grease on them, a mighty likely gal moved into town. She was the niece of Brer Wolf, and it looked as if all the menfolks were after her. They'd go down to Brer Wolf's house in the swamp, they would, and they'd sit up and court the gal and enjoy themselves.

It went on this way until after a while, the mosquitoes began to get monstrous bad. Brer Fox, he went flying around Miss Wolf, and he sat there, he did, and ran on with her and fought mosquitoes just as big as life and twice what was natural.

At last Brer Wolf, he caught Brer Fox slapping and fighting the mosquitoes. With that, he up and took Brer Fox by the ear and led him out to the front gate, and when he got there, Brer Wolf allowed, he did, that no man who didn't have the good manners to put up with mosquitoes was going to come courting his niece. If Miss Wolf could live with them, then so could the menfolks.

Brer Wolf's House in the Swamp

Then Brer Coon, he came flying around the gal, but he hadn't been there scarcely at all before he began to knock at the mosquitoes. No sooner had he done this than Brer Wolf showed him the door.

Brer Mink, he came and tried his hand, yet he couldn't help fighting the mosquitoes, and Brer Wolf asked him out.

It went on this way until by and by, all the menfolks had been flying around Brer Wolf's gal except Brer Rabbit. And when Brer Rabbit heard what kind of treatment the other folks had been catching, he allowed to himself that he believed in his soul that he'd better go on down to Brer Wolf's house. He'd prove that he could outsit those mosquitoes if it was his last act.

No sooner said than done. Off he put—lickety-clickety, clickety-lickety—and it wasn't long before he was knocking at Brer Wolf's front door.

Old Sis Wolf, she put down her knitting, and she up and allowed, "Who's that?"

Miss Wolf, she was standing up there, primping before the looking glass, and she choked back a giggle, she did, and said, "Sh-h-h! My goodness, that's Brer Rabbit. I hear the gals say he's a mighty proper gentleman, and I hope you aren't going to sit there and run on like you almost always do when I've got company—about how much soap grease you done saved up and how many kittens the old cat's got. I get right ashamed sometimes, I do."

The gal, she checked herself in the looking glass a time or two before she tiptoed to the door and opened it a little ways and peeped out. There stood Brer Rabbit looking just as slick as a racehorse.

Miss Wolf, she laughed, she did, and hollered, "Why, law! It's Brer Rabbit, and we've been afraid it was someone who had no business around here!"

Old Sis Wolf, she looked over her spectacles and snickered, and she up and allowed, "Well, don't keep him standing out there all night. Ask him in, for goodness sake."

Then the gal, she dropped her handkerchief, and Brer Rabbit, he dipped down and grabbed it and passed it to her with a bow. Miss Wolf said she was much obliged, because it was more than Brer Fox had done, and then Brer Rabbit asked her where Brer Wolf was. Old Sis Wolf allowed that she would go find him.

Bier Rabbit, a-Callin'

It wasn't long before Brer Rabbit heard Brer Wolf stomping the mud off of his feet in the back porch, and by and by, in he came. They shook hands, they did, and Brer Rabbit said that when he went calling on his acquaintances, it didn't feel natural unless the man of the house was sitting around somewhere.

"Even if he doesn't talk," said Brer Rabbit, said he, "he can just sit up against the chimney and keep time by nodding."

But old Brer Wolf, he was one of those men that got the whimzies, and he up and allowed that he didn't let himself get to nodding in front of company. They ran on this way until by and by, Brer Rabbit heard the mosquitoes come zooming around.

Brer Rabbit, he knew he had to do some mighty nice talking, so he up and asked for a drink of water. Miss Wolf, she up and fetched it.

"Mighty nice water." (*The mosquitoes, they zoomed.*)

"Some say it's too full of wiggle-tails, Brer Rabbit." (*The mosquitoes, they zoomed and zoomed.*)

"Mighty nice place you got." (*The mosquitoes, they zoomed.*)

"Some say it's too low in the swamp, Brer Rabbit." (*The mosquitoes, they zoomed, and they zoomed.*)

Those mosquitoes, they zoomed so bad that Brer Rabbit began to get scared, and when that rabbit gets scared, his mind works faster than a waterwheel.

By and by, he said, "Went to town the other day, and I saw a sight that I never expected to see."

"What's that, Brer Rabbit?"

"A spotted horse, Brer Wolf."

"*No,* Brer Rabbit."

"I most surely saw him, Brer Wolf."

Brer Wolf, he scratched his head, and the gal, she held up her hands and made great admiration about the spotted horse. (*The mosquitoes, they zoomed, and they kept on zooming.*)

"Let alone that, Brer Wolf, my granddaddy was spotted," said Brer Rabbit, said he.

The gal, she squealed and hollered out, "Why, Brer Rabbit! Aren't you ashamed of yourself to be talking that way about your own blood kin?"

Old Sis Wolf

Miss Meadows' Place

MAYBE you've heard talk about Miss Meadows and the gals, and about how Brer Rabbit was visiting there so much. Well, it happened that the lady friend Brer Rabbit had his eye on was one of the gals. He was sort of glad about it all at the off-start, but by and by, he began to get droopy. He laid around and sat about, he did, and he looked like he was studying something or another way off yonder.

It went on this way until by and by, Miss Meadows, she up and asked Brer Rabbit what in the name of sense was the matter with him, and Brer Rabbit, he felt so bad that he up and said, he did, that he was dead in love with one of the gals.

Then Miss Meadows, she up and asked him why he didn't tell the gal that he wanted to be a bridegroom. Brer Rabbit said he was ashamed.

Miss Meadows, she threw back her head, she did, and allowed, "I declare, you do look ashamed, now don't you? You might have been ashamed before hens had their teeth pulled out, but you haven't been

Brer Rabbit, in Love

ashamed since. I've seen you cut too many capers; I know there isn't a gal on the top side of the earth that can faze you," said Miss Meadows, said she.

Then Brer Rabbit allowed that he was scared the gal wouldn't have him, but Miss Meadows refused to confab with him anymore. She just broke out singing and washed the dishes, and what with the tune and the clatter of the dishes, Brer Rabbit couldn't hear past his own ears. By and by, he snuck out, he did, and went and sat by the spring.

He hadn't been sitting there long before Miss Molly Cottontail came by. This was the gal he'd been stewing about. She had a pail in her hand, and she was coming after water. She sashayed down the path, swinging the pail and singing.

Brer Rabbit had been feeling mighty droopy and low-spirited all morning, but as soon as he heard the gal singing, he fixed up his ears and looked sassy, and when she stopped singing, he broke out and began to sing himself.

Well, Miss Molly heard Brer Rabbit singing, and she sort of tossed her head and giggled. Brer Rabbit, he looked at her sideways and grinned.

Then Brer Rabbit allowed, "Morning, ma'am. How are you this fine day?"

The gal said, "I'm just tolerable. How do you do yourself?"

Brer Rabbit allowed, he did, "I thank you, ma'am, I'm right poorly. I haven't been feeling really pert in mighty near a month."

Miss Molly laughed and said, "That's what I hear tell. I expect you're in love, Brer Rabbit. You ought to go off somewhere and get yourself a wife."

This made Brer Rabbit feel sort of ashamed, and he hung his head and made marks in the sand with his foot. By and by, he said, "How is it, ma'am, that you don't get married?"

The gal laughed worse and worse, and after she caught her breath, she allowed, "Lordy, Brer Rabbit! I've got too much sense *myself* to be getting married without a sign or a dream."

Then Brer Rabbit said, "What kind of sign do you want, ma'am?"

The gal allowed, "Just any kind of sign; it doesn't make any difference what it is. I've tried all the spells, and I haven't seen a sign yet."

Miss Molly

Brer Rabbit said, "What kind of spells have you tried, ma'am?"

The gal allowed, "There's no telling, Brer Rabbit. I've tried everything I've heard about. I flung a ball of yarn out the window at midnight, and nobody came to wind it. I took a looking glass and looked down the well, and I didn't see anything at all. I took a hard-boiled egg and scooped the yellow out, and I filled it with salt and ate it without drinking any water. Then I went to bed, but I didn't dream about a blessed soul. I went out between sunset and dark and flung hemp seed over my left shoulder, but I haven't seen any beau yet."

Brer Rabbit, he allowed, he did, "If you'd told me when you were going, ma'am, I promise you'd have seen a beau."

Miss Molly, she giggled and said, "Oh hush, Brer Rabbit! If you don't go away from here, I don't know what I'll do! You're too funny for anything. What beau do you expect I'd have seen?"

Brer Rabbit, he up and allowed, he did, "You'd have seen me, ma'am. That's who you'd have seen."

The gal, she looked at Brer Rabbit just like her feelings were being hurt and said, "Aren't you ashamed of yourself, to be talking that way and making fun? I'm going away from this spring because it isn't any place for me."

With that, Miss Molly fetched her frock a flirt and went up the path like the dogs were on her trail.

She went so quick and so fast that she left her pail behind, and Brer Rabbit, he filled it with water and carried it on up to the house where Miss Meadows and the gals lived.

Then he came on back to the spring, and he sat there and studied and studied. He pulled his whiskers and scratched his head, and by and by, after he'd been sitting there a mighty long time, he jumped up and cracked his heels together, and then he laughed fit to kill himself.

He allowed, "You want a sign, do you? Well, I'm going to give you one, ma'am, and if that doesn't suit you, I'll give you more than one."

Miss Molly was gone, but Brer Rabbit, he hung around there, he did, and he lay his plans. When the dark came, he had them all fixed. The first thing that he did, he went down to the cane field, and there he found himself a long reed like you'd make into a fishing pole. After that, he hollowed it out from end to end.

Miss Meadows

When darkness came, Brer Rabbit took his cane and made his way to the house where Miss Meadows and the gals lived. He crept up, he did, and listened, and he heard them talking and laughing inside. It seemed like they had finished supper, and they were sitting around the fireplace.

By and by, Miss Molly said, "What do you reckon? I saw Brer Rabbit down by the spring."

Another gal said, "What was he doing down there?"

Miss Molly said, "I expect he was going gallivanting. He most surely did look mighty slick."

The other gal said, "I'm mighty glad to hear that, because the last time I saw him, it looked like his britches needed patching."

This talk made Brer Rabbit kind of solemn. But Miss Molly she up and allowed, "Well, he didn't look that way today, bless you! He looked as fine as one of those town chaps that you see come out of the Hominy Grove meetinghouse."

Miss Meadows, she heaved a sigh, she did, and said, "Fine or not fine, I wish Brer Rabbit or some other man or woman would come and wash up these dishes, because my back is so stiff I can scarcely stand up straight."

Then they all giggled, but Miss Molly said, "You all shan't talk about Brer Rabbit behind his back. He said he's going to be my beau."

Miss Meadows, she allowed, "Well, you'd better take him and make something or somebody out of him."

Miss Molly laughed and said, "Oh, no! I told him that before I get married, I've got to have some sign, so I'll know for sure when the time's come."

When Brer Rabbit heard this, he got in a big hurry. He took one end of the rod and stuck it in the crack of the chimney, and then he ran to the other end, which was out in the weeds. When he got there, he held it up to his head and listened, and he could hear them just as plain as if they were standing next to him.

Miss Meadows asked Miss Molly what kind of sign she wanted, and Miss Molly said she didn't care what kind it was, so long as it was a sign. Just then, Brer Rabbit put his mouth to the reed, and he talked like he had a bad cold.

Min Molly & Brer Rabbit by the Big Pine

He sang out, he did, "I want the gal who's after a sign!"

Miss Meadows said, "Who's that out there?"

Then they got a light and hunted all around the place and under the house, but they didn't see a thing.

They went back and sat down, they did, but it wasn't long before Brer Rabbit sang out, "I want the gal, and she must be mine!"

Miss Meadows and the gals were so astonished that they didn't know what to do, and by and by, Brer Rabbit, he sang out again:

I want the gal who's after a sign,
I want the gal, and she must be mine —
She'll see her beau down by the big pine.

And sure enough, the next morning when Miss Molly went down by the big pine, there sat Brer Rabbit, just as natural as life. The gal, she made out, she did, that she just came down there after a chaw of resin. They hemmed and hawed around right smart, disputing about this and that with one another.

But Brer Rabbit, he got the gal.

In Love for a Day

Music by Van Dyke Parks
Words by Van Dyke Parks and Martin F. Kibbee